Time FOR A Story

Focus on the Family
compiled & edited by *Joe Wheeler*

HARVEST HOUSE PUBLISHERS
EUGENE, OREGON 97402

Time for a Story

Copyright © 1999 Joe Wheeler
Published by Harvest House Publishers
Eugene, Oregon 97402

Focus on the Family® is a registered trademark of
Focus on the Family, Colorado Springs, CO 80995.
For more information, please contact

Focus on the Family
Colorado Springs, CO 80995
1-800-A-Family
www.family.org

Library of Congress Cataloging-in-Publication Data

Time for a Story / compiled and edited by Joe Wheeler.
        p.   cm.
    "A Focus on the Family book."
    Contents: Birthdays are lovely — At the eleventh hour / Eunice Creager — How Patty earned her salt / W.L. Colby — The widened hearth / Fannie H. Kilborne — Joseph's coat.
    Summary: Five stories, excerpted from "Great Stories Remembered," meant to teach Christian values to readers.
    ISBN 0-7369-0032-2
    1. Children's stories, American. [1. Christian life Fiction.
2. Short stories.] I. Wheeler, Joe L., 1936-   .
    PZ5. T45623 1999
    [Fic]—dc21

99-12779
CIP

This book has been excerpted from *Great Stories Remembered*, compiled and edited by Joe L. Wheeler (Focus on the Family Publishing, 1996).

"Birthdays Are Lovely," Author unknown. Published in *The Youth's Instructor*, July 24, 1928. Reprinted by permission of Review and Herald Publishing, Hagerstown, Maryland 21740.

"At the Eleventh Hour," by Eunice Creager. Published in *The Youth's Instructor*, April 18, 1916. Reprinted by permission of Review and Herald Publishing, Hagerstown, Maryland 21740.

"How Patty Earned Her Salt," by W.L. Colby. Published in *The Youth's Instructor*, July 22, 1913. Reprinted by permission of Review and Herald Publishing, Hagerstown, Maryland 21740.

"The Widened Hearth," by Fannie H. Kilbourne. If anyone can provide knowledge of the first publication source of this story, please relay this information to Joe L. Wheeler, care of Harvest House Publishers.

"Joseph's Coat." Author unknown. Published in *The Youth's Instructor*, November 19, 1929. Reprinted by permission of Review and Herald Publishing, Hagerstown, Maryland 21740.

Scripture verses are from the Holy Bible, New International Version ®. Copyright © 1973, 1978, 1984 by the International Bible Society. Used by permission of Zondervan Publishing House.

Design and production by Koechel Peterson and Associates, Minneapolis, Minnesota

Printed in the United States of America.

99 00 01 02 03 04 05 06 07 08 / IP / 10 9 8 7 6 5 4 3 2 1

CONTENTS

Tell Me a Story...

Stories...they are as old as time itself. Our conversation fairly swims in them:

"What did I do this weekend?...Oh, wait till you hear what happened to me! You see, I'd just locked the house when suddenly..."

"How was my day?...Oh, Mom! You'll never believe it—that new boy at school, he..."

"What happened to my hair? Well, my hair stylist was having a bad day and..."

Stories. We speak in stories to each other.

Why use stories? Perhaps because they alone remain in conscious, easy-to-access memory. I have long since forgotten most of what I have been exposed to in life, but my mother's stories are a part of my psyche, who I am, and hence key factors in how I live, how I treat people, how I perceive God.

I have become convinced, beyond a shadow of a doubt, that few things have a greater potential for good, for enrichment, for developing values, for creating empathy, for instilling kindness into the hearts, souls, and minds of children than does reading out loud to them.

And few more enduring bonds can exist on this planet than those created by reading to a child nestled on your lap or one encircled by your arm.

So turn off the television for the evening and enjoy reading the stories in this book with your family. You'll be richly rewarded.

Joe Wheeler

Birthdays
ARE
Lovely

AUTHOR UNKNOWN

Polly had never heard

of birthdays before…

so when one finally came,

she didn't really know

what people did with them.

olly was a dear girl who lived on a large farm with plenty of chickens, cows, and horses; but Polly never thought much about how nice all these were, for her father and mother were always hard at work. The two brothers worked with their father; her sister helped her mother in the house; and Polly washed the dishes, scoured the knives, fed the chickens, and ran errands for the family, and for all the summer boarders besides.

One of the boarders, Miss Cary, was watching Polly shell peas one morning and thinking that she did a great deal of work for such a little girl. Finally, she asked, "How old are you, Polly?"

"Eight," Polly answered.

"You're almost nine," said her mother.

"When is her birthday?" asked Miss Cary.

"Why, let me see; it's this month sometime—the seventeenth of July. I declare, I'd have forgotten all about it if you hadn't spoken." And Mrs. Jones went on with her work again.

"What's a birthday?" Polly asked shyly.

"Why, Polly," exclaimed Miss Cary, "don't you know? It's the anniversary of the day you were born. Didn't you ever have a birthday present, Polly?"

"No," said Polly, looking puzzled.

"We never have much time for these things," Polly's mother said. "It's about all I can do to remember Christmas."

"Yes, I know," Miss Cary said, but she resolved that Polly should have a birthday.

When she came down to breakfast the morning of the seventeenth, Miss Cary met Polly in the hall and, putting a little purse into her hand, said kindly, "Here, Polly, is something for you to buy birthday presents with."

Polly opened the little bag and found in it nine bright silver quarters. She ran as fast as she could to tell her mother.

"Why, child!" her mother said, "that's too much money for you to spend. Better save it. It will help buy you a pair of shoes and a warm dress next winter."

Almost any girl would have cried at this, and Polly's eyes did fill with tears; but as her mother wanted her to help "put the breakfast on," she took the plate of muffins into the dining room.

Miss Cary noticed the wet lashes and said, "Mrs. Jones, please let Polly go down to the stores today and spend her birthday money."

Mrs. Jones could not refuse this request. So after she had put the baby to sleep, Polly was allowed to go down to the village, which was a good two miles away, all by herself. The happy girl would have willingly walked five miles to spend her precious money.

It was late in the afternoon when she came back. The boarders were lounging about, waiting for the supper bell to ring. They all smiled at the little figure toiling up the road, with her arms full of bundles.

Polly smiled back radiantly through the dust that covered her round little face as she called to Miss Cary, "Oh, I've got lots of things! Please come into the kitchen and see."

"No, it's too warm there," Miss Cary said. "Come into the living room, where it's cool, and we can all see."

So they went into the house, and Polly began to unwrap her packages and exhibit her purchases.

"There," she said as she tore the paper from an odd-shaped bundle. "This is for Mother"—she held up an eggbeater—"'cause it takes so long to beat eggs with a fork."

The boarders looked at each other in surprise, but Polly was too busy to notice.

She fairly beamed as she held up a green glass necktie pin for inspection. "Isn't it lovely?" she said. "It's for Father."

"This isn't much," she continued, opening a small bundle, "only a rattle for Baby. It cost five cents."

The boarders looked on in silence as the busy little fingers untied strings. No one knew whether to laugh or feel sorry.

It was wonderful what nine quarters would buy, and not strange that the little girl had spent a whole half day shopping. There was a blue tie for brother Dan, and a pink one for Tim; a yellow hair ribbon for sister Linda; some hairpins for Grandma; and a small bottle of cologne for Jake, the "hired man." Then there was but one package left. Polly patted this lovingly as she opened it.

"This is the nicest of all, and it's for you," she said as she handed Miss Cary a box of pink writing paper. "It seemed too bad that you only had plain white paper to write on, when you write so lovely. So I got you this. Isn't it pretty?"

"Why, it's beautiful, Polly dear," Miss Cary said, "but what have you bought for your birthday present?"

"Why, these," said Polly, "these are all my presents. Presents are something we give away, aren't they?" And Polly looked around, wondering why all were so still.

"It is more blessed to give than to receive," said one of the boarders softly, and Miss Cary put her arms around Polly and kissed the hot, dusty little face again and again.

"It's been a lovely day," Polly said. "I never had any presents to give away before, and I think birthdays are just lovely."

The next month, after Miss Cary returned to the city, *she* had a birthday; and there came to Polly a most wonderful doll, with beautiful clothes, and a card saying, "For Polly, on my birthday, from Lena Cary" which, by the way, immediately became the doll's name.

Miss Cary was not the only one who caught Polly's idea of a birthday. The rest of the boarders remembered, and through the year, as each one's birthday came, Polly received a gift to delight her generous little heart.

When the seventeenth of July came around again, Miss Cary was not on the farm, but she sent Polly a little silk bag with 10 silver quarters in it—and Polly still thinks "birthdays are lovely."

A generous man will
himself be blessed ...

PROVERBS 22:9

AT THE
Eleventh Hour

EUNICE CREAGER

Both Milly and Gertrude

desperately wanted

that teaching job.

There wasn't much Milly

wouldn't do to get it. . . .

"Mrs. Miller said the choice of the school board lies between you and Gertrude Dosch, Milly. Of course it was told confidentially. You must not repeat this."

Milly looked up from the big dictionary she was studying. Her effort at a smile was rather pitiful. "Well, that's an advantage, anyway, isn't it, Mother?" she said, laughing cheerfully. "A race with only one."

"In my judgment, it is not much of a race, Milly. Gertrude's work has been brilliant, but careless; you have built on solid foundations. You are by far the better student and more deserving of it."

"Oh, Mother! How can you say that?" objected Milly nervously, trying to keep a sob out of her voice. "I see so many questions in these old teachers' examinations that I do not know! To think of Gertrude always having help like this! She must know all the answers. How I wish I could have had them a month or two ago!"

"She probably never looked at them much. It was good of her to lend them to you, though."

"She couldn't help it," remarked Milly dryly. "I asked her for them."

"And the dictionary—did she lend you that?"

"No. She has one, but she would never have offered it. Besides, she would need it for her own reference work. Philip Brooks insisted on bringing me his this afternoon. You were uptown. He said it would be helpful, and it certainly is."

The telephone rang suddenly, insistently. "I'll answer it, Mother. I think it is one of the girls. Hello!"

Gertrude's voice at the other end of the line answered happily. "Hello! Are you going tonight?"

"No, I'm not going, Gertrude."

"Now what's the matter, Milly? Studying, I'll warrant you! Catch me poring over my books! Well, I'll have to get on my new dress. Oh, it is a perfect dream of yellow and white. I am wild about it."

Milly hung up the receiver and met the questioning eyes of her mother.

"What is it, Milly? Was there a party tonight? Why aren't you going?" Then an understanding look crept into the mother's tired, faded eyes. "I feel sure I could have made the blue silk presentable if you had told me in time."

"It wasn't that altogether, Mother," Milly said truthfully. "I felt that while I had the back numbers of these teachers' magazines, I should make use of them and lose no time. It is only two days now until the teachers' examination." Then, as she noticed her mother's drawn face, she cried out: "Oh, do put up your sewing and go to bed, Mother! You look so tired. You have done enough for two persons today. Do put it up," she coaxed, bending over her mother's chair, "and, oh, Mumsie, pray for me tonight!"

Mrs. Benton gave her daughter a quick look and held out her arms. Milly jumped into them. "There, there! You are all nervous and unstrung. Pray for you? I have prayed for you, child, every night since you entered the world. That's what mothers are for. I think you will get the place; but if you don't, it will be only a matter of time. Don't worry, Milly. We will pull through some way. Good night, and don't sit up too late."

Milly sat down at the library table littered with teachers' magazines and the big dictionary with a firm determination to keep her mind on her study.

On the day of the teachers' examination, Milly walked briskly toward the courthouse, in which the examination was to be held. Strangely enough, her former nervousness had vanished, and in its place was a calm confidence, the result, probably, of a good night's sleep. The night of the party, Milly had read questions and answers until her brain whirled; then, with a remnant of sanity remaining, she had closed the books and put them out of sight. "I will not look at them another time," she declared. "'Tis true I haven't a library or help like these magazines, but all my life I have been a better student than Gertrude. Why should I cloud my brain by cramming at the last? I will not look up another thing!"

As the result of this wisdom, Milly's brain was never clearer than when she took her seat and began work. A glance at the morning subjects sent a thrill of exultation through her. Gertrude, across the aisle, was writing rapidly and confidently. Milly began what she knew would be good work.

The morning passed quickly, and 12:00 came. As the papers were handed in, Milly stopped at Gertrude's desk. "Are you ready to go now, Gertrude?" she inquired pleasantly.

"I am not going home for dinner. I am going across the street to Aunt Linda's," answered Gertrude, avoiding Milly's eyes and making no effort to rise.

Milly, with a puzzled look, passed out of the room. At the door, Mr. Baxter, the county superintendent, held out a cordial hand. "I must congratulate you, Miss Benton, on your good work this morning. I have been looking over your paper."

"Oh, thank you, Mr. Baxter. But I may meet my Waterloo this afternoon. History is what I fear."

"You have cause," the superintendent answered quickly. "It is the stiffest examination I have ever known."

Milly went slowly down the courthouse steps, her high spirits a little dampened by this news. A crowd of girls, school aspirants, flocked down the steps ahead of her, their voices floating back.

"Oh, we can't hope to get the place at the main building if we do pass. That lies between Gertrude Dosch and Milly Benton. All we can hope for is a country school. They say it is hard for the school board to choose between them, and that they are waiting to see who passes the better examination before they decide."

"Won't Gertrude splurge if she gets it? She said she wanted it because then she could buy more pretty clothes."

"Whew-who-ah! Whew-who-ah!" Will Martin's peculiar and familiar whistle rang out. Milly smiled and waited. "Say, have pity on a fellow, will you? I've been trying to catch up ever since you left the courthouse. Guess what I have in my pocket."

"Couldn't guess," said Milly, dimpling.

Will's laughter was always infectious. "The examination questions, Milly—none other."

Milly gave a startled exclamation.

"Baxter gave them to my business college last night. Of course they gave them to me with the understanding that I let no one see them, but mum's the word, Milly. I know how you dread history, and it's a hard one, too, I'll tell you. Here, take them! No one will ever know."

Will held out the papers, and for one brief moment that seemed like years, Milly wavered. She thought of the three hard years since her father's death; how her mother had struggled, baking, sewing, ironing, working beyond her strength to get her through school; of her mother's physical breakdown in the last few months. She *must* have that school. It not only meant bread and butter, but also medical attention for her mother.

On the other hand, this thing she was contemplating meant the upheaval of all her years of training. She remembered her mother's face and the look in her eyes when she said, "Pray for you? Why, child, I have prayed for you every night since you entered the world."

"I can't do it, Will," she said, quietly. "Thanks, but I can't do it."

"Oh, come! You don't mean it," coaxed Will, a quizzical expression in his eyes.

Milly turned away with an air of finality. "Yes, I am in earnest."

"Well, good-bye, then! Good luck to you. Not many would have turned down that offer, Milly."

Milly thought so herself as she watched Will, with the coveted history questions, swing jauntily down the street.

The history examination more than justified the rumor of "stiff." Milly's heart sank as she looked at the questions; but pushing them in the background of her mind, she went to work on the other subjects and soon had finished them to her satisfaction.

Across the aisle, Gertrude took her history questions and calmly wrote "History" at the top of her paper. Ah, she was ready, too!

Milly sat in her seat and chewed her pencil in a vain effort to answer question number one. Gertrude wrote calmly and confidently on. Indeed, the steady scribble of Gertrude's pencil began to get on Milly's nerves. How did it come that Gertrude found the questions so easy to answer? She had always been weaker in history than Milly.

At last, hot and exasperated, Milly was forced to hand in her paper with two questions unanswered. Sick at heart, she turned her steps homeward.

Gertrude, calm and cool in her green linen, had left the courthouse an hour before. Milly walked on, a sense of utter failure weighting her limbs. She felt suddenly old and tired. A lump rose in her throat. History had spoiled everything for her. Even if she answered the other questions correctly, she could not hope for anything higher than 80 percent.

Mrs. Benton was not at home, for which Milly was truly thankful; it gave her an opportunity to indulge in a good cry.

A few days later, Milly was returning from town when Lulu Thaxter overtook her. "Milly," she began anxiously, "have you put in your application for a country school?"

Milly smiled ruefully. "Yes, I did, the day after the teachers' examination."

"Look here, Milly, there's something odd about that," said Lulu, lowering her voice. "Gertrude answered every question in the examination correctly. What do you know about that? I went to Uncle William's to look up a reference in their library. You know he is on the school board. There were voices in the other room. I did not pay any attention until your name was mentioned. Before I realized what I was doing, I had heard a lot that was not intended for me. They all agreed that your papers were better, but two of the history questions were blank. Did you forget them, honey?"

"No," groaned Milly. "I simply didn't know them, Lulu."

"Well, Mr. Baxter met with the board, and he was strong for you. He said, aside from the two questions left blank, yours were the finest set of papers he had ever examined; and although your grade was lower than Gertrude's, he recommended you to the school board. Well, they disagreed. Uncle William Miller stood firm for you, while Mr. Wells and Mr. Thompson wanted to give the place to Gertrude. You know it's all mixed up with politics some way. Unfortunately, Mr. Baxter couldn't vote, and the majority ruled, and the school went to Gertrude. Oh, Milly, I could just cry! But don't mind, for Mr. Baxter said the country trustee would give you the best school he had if you wanted it."

The best country school he had! Milly turned this over in her mind as she left Lulu and walked slowly homeward. Even the best, with board taken out, was a pitifully small amount of money. It meant another year of hard work for her mother, who was at the breaking point now. It was a bitter disappointment.

"Well, Mother, I guess it's a sure thing I shall be a country school-ma'am," remarked Milly that night, smiling at her mother, although tears were fighting for mastery; and she repeated the story to her mother.

Mrs. Benton's pale face whitened, but that was the only sign. "Never mind, Milly. It will be only a question of time. Have patience, dear. You are so young; the country school will give you experience."

"Experience, yes, but not much money. We need the money so, Mother. I had thought…" Milly's voice, trailed off pitifully.

"Never mind, darling. Don't lose your fine sense of values. I know we are poor and need money badly, but all the money in the world would not satisfy me if you were weak and shallow like some girls. I thank God every night for the strength of character of my dear girl. As long as I have this knowledge and the knowledge of our love for each other, I can work hard with a light heart, for I have something better than money."

"Oh, Mother, how could anyone be very bad and live with you? But does it always pay to do right, I wonder?"

"Always. What a strange question for you to ask, Milly. What is it?"

"Nothing, only—oh, sometimes it seems that the one who does wrong gets the best of everything."

"Not for long," declared Mrs. Benton gravely. "The one who does right wins in the end."

On the morning of the day the assignments were to be published, Milly was uptown trying to match some braid for her mother. She was thinking of Gertrude and what joy the day would bring her, and wondering, too, why she had not seen her lately. Glancing out of the window, she saw Gertrude and Will Martin coming out of Dr. Miller's office. Will looked red and excited, and Gertrude was weeping bitterly.

Milly's heart gave a quick throb of pity. *Mrs. Dosch is worse*, she thought quickly. Gertrude's mother had not been well all summer. *Here I was, half envying her, and perhaps she is in terrible trouble.* After a vain attempt to overtake them, Milly decided she would telephone and ask about Gertrude's mother; but when she got home, her own mother was so ill from a severe headache that it drove the incident from her mind.

By afternoon Mrs. Benton was suffering so much that Milly started to Dr. Miller's office to get medicine. The old man looked up as she entered and grunted a good afternoon. "How's the schoolma'am?" he said teasingly.

"All right—if I am one. But Mother needs some more medicine for her head, Doctor."

The old man rose stiffly and went behind the counter. He often filled his own prescriptions. Milly leaned over the counter. "Tell me which school I got," she coaxed. "Will you, Dr. Miller? Do you know?"

The doctor set the big glass jar down on the counter and regarded her with jovial eyes. He winked. "Milly, did you ever meet Old Nick on the street in broad daylight?" he asked; and then, as if in answer to the amazement in Milly's eyes, he went on, his little eyes twinkling: "On the street, in the guise of a friend with a—well, let's say examination questions in his pocket?"

Watching Milly closely and observing the look of understanding leap to her eyes, the fat old man laughed out loud. "But Will, unlike Old Nick, doesn't know how to keep a still tongue. He talks too much," chuckled the doctor. "I got a whiff of the news and brought him in here, but he wouldn't talk, not he—stubborn as an old mule. Then I went for Gertrude; that brings them to time."

"Gertrude?" gasped Milly. "What has she to do with it?"

"Hoity-toity!" laughed the old man, thoroughly enjoying himself. "Don't think you're the only one! You're second choice, Milly. Gertrude was first choice, and she fell for them. Guess his conscience got to hurting him some, so he had to offer them to you, too. Well, I got them both in here. Will blustered and Gertrude cried, but I got the truth out of them

25

all right. Thought it was odd she came out with such flying colors. Talk about many a slip 'twixt cup and lip! Why, the girl had that school.

"Well, I did some quick work. That school board was here in a jiffy, and I stated my case. It was easy sailing after that. The tide turned, as I knew it would, and you have the place at the main building. Gertrude hasn't any. I tell you, we had to hustle, though, to get those names changed at the *Herald* office. We were just in time."

During the recital, Milly had run the gamut of emotions. "Pinch me," she said finally. "I must be dreaming."

The doctor's eyes softened. "It is no dream, child. Here are the powders. Run home and tell your mother. I know what it means to you." Waving aside her thanks—he hurried the bewildered girl out of his office.

Once outside, Milly almost ran along the street, so eager was she to get home with the glad news. As she sped past Brooks's store, Philip Brooks ran out, waving a paper. "Wait a minute! Congratulations, Milly."

"Oh, Philip, is that tonight's *Herald*? Let me see it."

Smiling at Milly's eagerness, Philip handed her the paper. There it was in big headlines: "Miss Benton Gets Place at Main Building." Milly read it with dancing eyes and cheeks aglow.

"Wait while I get my hat," said Philip, "and I'll take you home in the car; it's about supper time anyway."

In a moment, they were spinning rapidly down the street and were soon at Milly's home. Milly danced happily up the steps and into her mother's room. "Oh, Mother, you were right! You are always right," she cried joyously. "I've won! I've won!"

The good man will
be rewarded for his ways.

PROVERBS 14:14

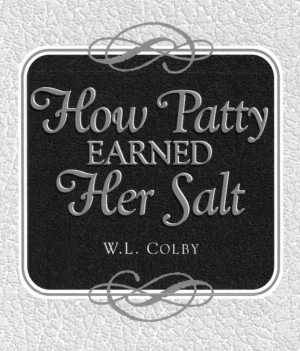

How Patty EARNED Her Salt

W.L. Colby

Things aren't always
what they seem —
and neither are people.

"S he doesn't even earn her own salt," Patty had heard her mother say that morning in an impatient tone. "If she were only a boy, now, she might run errands or do something to get a little money, and we need every cent we can get, with the interest money to be paid, and land knows what else!"

"Tut, tut, child!" replied the good old Quaker grandmother. "Thee must remember, Sophia, that the little one's a mere chick yet and can only pick up the bits the mother hen scratches for." And Mrs. Drake, without saying more, had gone about her work, all unconscious that her words had been heard by the little girl beneath the window.

Poor Patty! How those words kept repeating themselves in her ears! Was it true that she did not earn her salt? And she was so fond of salt. Her father often laughingly remarked that Patty would probably want to salt her coffee when she grew to be a woman.

How she wished she were a boy! Then, as her mother had said, she might earn some money by doing errands. Only the day before, the boy who came to deliver the groceries had told Patty's mother that old Miss Hunter wanted a boy to run errands for her. "But," he added, "she's so awful stingy with her money that none of the boys will go near her."

Perhaps, though, thought Party, *she would be willing to give salt for pay.* And couldn't she run errands just as well as any boy? Her feet were good and strong, and didn't she walk three-quarters of a mile each day to school and back?

Patty resolved, in spite of all the stories she had heard about the stingy old woman, that she would go and ask Miss Hunter to let her do the errands for her; although her little heart beat like a triphammer at the very thought of so bold an undertaking.

Miss Hunter lived in an old-fashioned mansion, only a short distance from the unpretentious farmhouse of the Drakes. Her brother had been a much respected squire in the quiet town and was supposed to have been wealthy. But when he died, leaving his place to his only sister, Miss Hunter immediately dismissed two of the servants, retaining only one old man, who was lame and very deaf, to do the chores, while she occupied one room and seemed determined to have nothing to do with anyone.

The only time she was to be seen on the street was on Sundays, when she drove to church in the strange old chaise behind the dismal-looking horse, which won for itself the title of "Old Calamity." She never went to the store herself, and if a peddler were so bold as to call at her door, he was ordered away at once with the remark, "Don't come near me with your trash; I can't afford it!"

Patty had seen her in church—sitting always in the same position, never moving a muscle of her face until the sermon was over—when she would take her spectacles off, put them into their case, and walk out in a slow, dignified manner, speaking to no one and looking neither to the right nor the left.

Such was the woman Patty had determined to serve. Was it any wonder her heart failed her? But as often as she felt like giving up her enterprise, her mother's words "She doesn't even earn her salt" would ring in her ears, giving her fresh determination.

Accordingly the next day, on her way home from school, Patty walked bravely up the weed-grown path and knocked on the front door with the great brass knocker, which represented a lion holding a ring in his mouth. If the lion's head had been a live one, Patty would scarcely have stood more in fear of it.

It seemed to her hours before she heard any sound, and not daring to knock again, she made up her mind to give up the attempt and go home, when she heard a scraping sound as of a huge bolt being slid, and the door was opened a little.

"No, we don't want anything today," exclaimed a squeaky voice, "we've got all the pins and needles we want, and—"

"If you please, ma'am, I don't want to sell anything," answered Patty, breaking in on the old lady's speech, fearful lest the door would be closed before she could make known her errand. "I'm Patty Drake, who lives in the house just a little way down the road, and I've come to ask you—"

"You needn't come here begging," began the old lady in a sharp tone of voice. "We have enough to do to take care of ourselves without—"

"But, if you please, ma'am, I don't want to beg for anything, either," again broke in Patty. "Only I heard the other day that you wanted a boy to do errands for you, and so I thought—that maybe—perhaps—I could do them for you."

"But you are not a boy," answered the old lady, opening the door a little wider.

"No'm, but I can walk just as well as a boy, and teacher says I've got a good mem'ry, and you'd only have to pay me in salt," replied Patty.

"Pay you in salt, child! What do you mean?" exclaimed the old lady, opening the door still wider to get a view of her visitor.

"Why, you see, ma'am, Mother said yesterday that I didn't even earn my salt, and I do like it so much, and I thought maybe you would let me do your errands for you and pay me in salt, and you could hang a towel from the window whenever you wanted me, just as Mother does when she wants the baker to stop, and I could do all the errands you would want done before and after school," answered the little girl almost in one breath, anxious to cover all possible objections at once.

"Well, well! I never!" muttered Miss Hunter. "How old are you, pray tell?"

"If you please, ma'am, I'm nine years old, going on ten."

"And do you think you could keep your own counsel, child?"

"If you please, what is it to keep your own counsel?" asked Patty.

"Why, it means that you mustn't tell people all that you see and hear in other folks' houses."

"Oh, I never do that!" exclaimed Patty. "Mother doesn't allow me to tell what I hear folks say, 'cause she says it's telling tales out of school, and I'm sure, if you would only let me do your errands for you, I would never tell anybody what I heard."

"Humph!" muttered Miss Hunter. "Your mother is more sensible than most people, and I guess," she continued, half-musing, "that this little girl is just the one I want; she's big enough to do small errands, and Jake can do all the large ones—which aren't many—and," turning to Patty, "so you would be willing to take pay in salt, would you?"

"Oh, yes'm, indeed I would!" she cried. "Will you—oh, will you let me?" Her eyes fairly danced at the prospect.

"Well, if Mother is willing, and you will be sure to do your work in good shape. You will have to watch sharp for the cloth I hang out when I want you. Mind, it won't do for you to be off playing every time I want you; and you know, above all, you are to keep your own counsel. Can you do an errand for me this afternoon?"

"I suppose," faltered Patty. "I ought to ask Mother first; but I know she will let me, and I will be right back." And suiting the action to her words, she sped away as fast as her feet could carry her.

Her mother was not at home, but in answer to Patty's breathless request that she might go and do something for Miss Hunter, the dear old grandmother, half-dozing in her chair, said "Yes." Patty scampered back, scarcely able to contain herself, and thinking all the time how pleased her mother would be when she would hear that her little girl was actually "earning her own salt."

Miss Hunter answered her knock, and handing her a covered basket, told her to take it to old Mrs. Brown, a poor, lame widow living at the end of a crossroad that ran between Patty's home and Miss Hunter's. "But mind," she added, "you are not to say anything about it to anybody." Patty assented, carrying the basket as she was bidden.

It did not take her long to do her errand. Then, as Miss Hunter said there was nothing else to do that day, she hurried home, eager to tell her mother the good news.

But she was doomed to disappointment. Her mother was indignant and declared that Patty should not be allowed to do any such thing. "The idea!" she exclaimed, "pay you in salt, indeed! No, she shan't, not if I know it."

But here the grandmother interposed. "And why not let the child do as she wishes, Sophia? Did not thee say but yesterday that Patty was good for naught at home, and if she does as the old lady desires she will not be doing mischief. She surely can do no harm, and who knows," she added, "but the little one's innocent ways may have a good effect on the old woman?" And at length Mrs. Drake yielded, as she always did, sooner or later, to her mother's calm reasoning.

So Patty entered regularly upon her duties as errand girl. To be sure, she did not have very much to do for the old lady, but then she was doing something and was no longer a useless being.

As time wore on, there grew a strange attachment between the old lady and Patty, and after a while it became quite an ordinary affair for Patty to stop at Miss Hunter's on her way home from school, even when the cloth was not hanging from the window. She delighted to step in and wash the dishes on a Saturday and to help Miss Hunter dust the rooms on sweeping day.

People wondered much at it, but Patty, true to her word, kept "her own counsel" and did not tell what she often longed to have others know: Oh! she did want so much, sometimes, to tell people that what they took for miserly actions were only self-denying for the sake of others. For Patty could have told of many a basket of needed things that went into the little cottage at the end of the lane. Many a time she had carried jellies and dainty dishes to the houses of sick, poor people, but always with instructions that the receiver must tell no one whence they came.

Strange as it may seem, for once, the village gossip was baffled; those who received favors from the old lady respected her whims and "kept their own counsel." True, some wag in the village jokingly remarked "that the old miser," pointing to Miss Hunter's house, "had grown so greedy that she sent a basket to collect the rent from some of her tenants," but no one knew the real facts of the case.

Patty might have told, too, about the weekly letter she carried to the post office containing money to pay the board of an old feeble-minded uncle in a distant, private hospital, simply because this same uncle had taken care of Miss Hunter when she was a little girl. She had resolved that as long as she lived, he should not want for a single comfort. This had been her principal reason for the economy of the fortune left her by the squire, which was far from being as large as people supposed.

Misjudged by others, the old lady kept on in her way, taking great comfort in her newfound friend, for such Patty proved to be. Patty, on her part, began to love the one who denied herself luxuries for the sake of others.

The summer wore away, and winter came on cold and severe. Patty's father met with several losses in succession. First, the barn burned down, then his two best cows died of a prevalent disease, and things began to look unusually discouraging. Worst of all, the interest on the mortgage would soon be due again.

Mrs. Drake complained bitterly of their "poor luck," and Patty, young as she was, shared the feeling of gloom and despair that hung over them, for no one knew what they would do, or where they would go, if they lost their home.

One morning, as Patty was starting to school, her father called her to him. "Are you going to stop at Miss Hunter's?" he asked.

"No, sir, but I'd just as soon; I shall have time enough."

"Well, I wish you would take this letter to her," and he added, "you might stop on your way home for an answer."

Patty took the letter and carried it as she was bidden, wondering much what it could be about, for her father did not often write a letter. What could he be writing to Miss Hunter for—was it something about her?

All day long her mind kept reverting to the letter, and she could hardly wait for school to be dismissed, so anxious was she to see Miss Hunter, in hopes that she might find out something about it.

When Miss Hunter opened the letter Patty left that morning and read it, she found just a few simple sentences, stating that the writer, George Drake, having met with severe losses, would be unable to pay the interest on the mortgage that was held by her, and asking for time to obtain the necessary money.

Although the day seemed very long to Patty, school at length came to a close, and she hastened as fast as possible to the old lady's house.

Miss Hunter answered her knock and invited her to come in. As it was very cold, the woman insisted that Patty should sit down by the fire and warm herself. For a little while they sat in silence, and then the old lady said, "Patty, do you remember the day you came and asked me to let you do my errands?"

"Yes'm."

"Have you forgotten what you told me you wanted for pay?"

"No'm."

"Why haven't you asked me for your pay?"

"Because I thought you would give it to me when you wanted to."

"Well, I've been thinking today," replied the old lady, "that it is about time you received some of your wages. You have been a good girl and have earned your salt well." So saying, she handed Patty a tin pail, which she said was full of salt.

"Be careful not to spill any, and be sure you bring back the pail, as I cannot spare it long," she admonished.

"Thank you ever so much," exclaimed Patty thinking how pleased her mother would be when she should show her that she had really earned something.

"Oh!" suddenly remembering her errand, "I was to call for an answer to the letter I left this morning."

"Never mind the answer tonight," replied Miss Hunter.

It seemed to Patty that the old lady had a beautiful expression on her face that she had never seen before, as she bade her good night.

She hurried home with her pail of salt, feeling very happy at the thought that it was all her own. But Mrs. Drake shared no such feeling; her indignation began, as usual, to rise, and it was an effort for her to control herself and keep from saying harsh things, which would have spoiled Patty's pleasure. What was a little pail of salt, compared with what Patty had done!

The tears sprang to her eyes. "And she even wants you to bring back the pail, doesn't she? The sting—" but a look from Patty made her pause. "Well, no matter, I'll empty it right away, and you can carry the pail back tomorrow morning. We are almost out of salt anyway—that's one comfort."

So saying, she carried the salt into the pantry.

In a moment they heard her utter an exclamation of surprise. "Mother! Patty!" she called. "Come here quick!"

They hurried into the pantry to see what could be the matter, and Mr. Drake, who was just bringing in the milk, joined them.

On the table was a pan into which Mrs. Drake had just poured the salt. But what was that glittering here and there in the pan? Gold; yes, gold coins—eagles, half-eagles, a number of smaller coins—all bright and shining, as if happy at the thought of the good they might do. And in an envelope was a gift of the mortgage on the house, presented to Patty Drake, from her friend Adeline Hunter, with these words: "You have earned your salt."

The work of a man's hands
rewards him.

PROVERBS 12:14

THE
Widened
Hearth

FANNIE H. KILBOURNE

A widow and her

teenage daughters

decide to reinvent

Thanksgiving Day.

"ouldn't you think they would be invited *some-where*?" Kathleen demanded. "Wouldn't you think even boarders would like to go out to dinner on *Thanksgiving*?"

"Couldn't we tell them that we don't serve meals on holidays?" Lois suggested.

Their mother shook her head. "It's never done. All boardinghouses have a big dinner on holidays."

"Oh, Mother," Lois protested, "please don't call this a boardinghouse! Having four paying guests doesn't make a place a boardinghouse."

"That which we call a rose—" Kathleen quoted lightly.

"Whatever you call it," their practical mother said, "it seems to bring its responsibilities."

"It isn't fair that being poor should keep us from having a home," said Lois. "It's bad enough having all the extra work, but it's having boarders around all the time that I mind. Home isn't home when it's full of strangers."

"It's bad enough to have boarders any time," Kathleen said, taking up the plaint, "but it does seem as if they might go away on holidays!"

Their four "paying guests" had been with the Martins for three months. Taking them had seemed the inevitable sequel to the Consolidated failure. During the long years of Mrs. Martin's widowhood, the check from the Consolidated had been one of the rocks of assurance on which her life was built.

Then the Consolidated failed, and the check stopped coming. It all happened with a suddenness and unexpectedness that stunned the Martins. For days Mrs. Martin was more bewildered and incredulous than she was frightened. But the fright followed soon enough. Never could she forget the terror of the hot July evening when she had finally accepted the fact that the Consolidated check would come no more and had taken account of her resources.

There was "home," an attractive 10-room stone house. Chestnut Avenue had been on the outskirts of town when Mrs. Martin had gone to the stone house as a bride 20 years ago. During the 20 years, the city had slowly crept up—a store building here, an apartment house there. Electric cars thundered up and down the next block, hotels and bakeries appeared on the cross streets; the neighborhood was only a few minutes' walk from the busiest part of the city—yet Chestnut Avenue stood alone, a shady, restful island of homes in the restless sea of traffic.

Besides home, the assets were few; the tiny income that was still coming would scarcely pay the coal bill and the taxes. Then there were the girls, Lois aged 17, Kathleen aged 15, still in high school, two lovable liabilities. Home was in a desirable part of the town, near business yet quiet. "Paying guests" offered the only solution to the problem.

"Well, if we've sunk to where we have to take boarders, we'll take them," Lois had said grimly. "We'll give them comfortable rooms and good food, but we won't—"

"Won't be clubby with them," Kathleen suggested.

"No, we won't," Lois had agreed. "They'll have their own lives, and we'll have ours. We won't let their being here spoil our home life."

The four boarders had been able to pay good prices for their large sunny rooms and appetizing meals; they knew nothing of the planning and penny-pinching behind the scenes. The Martins kept to themselves as much as possible, striving to maintain their means of livelihood on a formal, businesslike basis.

"We could fool ourselves all right before," Lois went on almost tearfully, "pretending keeping boarders didn't make any difference. But on holidays it shows up. We can't have people we'd like here for dinner with four strangers, and we can't go anywhere ourselves because we have to stay and get dinner for them."

"I thought surely Miss Dunn would be invited somewhere," Kathleen said. "Didn't you, Mother?"

"She expected to go home," Mrs. Martin explained, "and then, just last week, the schools decided to stay open Friday, so she can't go."

"I heard her refuse an invitation over the telephone just before she found out," said Lois.

"I suppose we ought to have a turkey," mused Mrs. Martin. "And turkey is 55 cents a pound. I wonder if we'll have to have soup?"

"We had five courses last year," Lois reminded them wistfully. "We won't have to bother with cheese, crackers, and candied orange peel and things like that this year, anyway. Isn't it funny how much more work it seems to be to get up a dinner for people you don't want than for people you do? I never think of the trouble of clearing up after a party, but the idea of washing the dishes after this dinner—well, I just wish Thanksgiving were over!"

"Girls!" cried Kathleen, suddenly straightening up and looking from one to the other with bright eyes. Kathleen always addressed her mother and sister in that collective way, which secretly delighted her quiet, practical mother. "Girls, let's make it a party. As long as we've lost our home anyway, let's get some fun out of it. Let's pretend we're giving a dinner party and have place cards and flowers and—well, maybe not flowers, but everything that is spiffy and cheap and—"

She paused enthusiastically, but her enthusiasm was not reflected in the faces of the other two.

"Getting up a big dinner is about all the work I want," sighed her mother.

"Oh, we'll do all the party part of it, won't we, Lois?" said Kathleen. "Oh, come on; it would be lots of fun. We haven't had a party since the Consolidated failed. Come on, please! It would be great fun!"

"I suppose I could paint the place cards myself," said Lois.

"We could send them invitations," Kathleen went on eagerly. "Of course, they'll come anyhow, but it would let them know that it was a party. We—"

"We'll use the gorgeous stationery Aunt Kate gave me for my birthday," said Lois.

"We can have alligator-pear salad," said Mrs. Martin, "if Uncle Will's box from Florida gets here in time. That is always considered as quite a delicacy."

"We'll have a fire in the grate," said Lois.

"And serve the coffee in front of it!" said Kathleen, suddenly inspired.

Enthusiasm had begun its leavening; already Thanksgiving dinner had begun to be a "party."

Tuesday evening a large square envelope lay at each boarder's place.

"Mrs. Anne Upland Martin and her daughters, Miss Lois and Miss Kathleen Martin, would be pleased to have you take dinner with them at 2:00 Thanksgiving Day and spend the afternoon, if there is nothing else that you want to do."

The message was of Kathleen's composing and was written in Lois's pretty hand. The four boarders read the missives through and then looked up.

"Well, I'll be tickled to death," said pretty little Miss Dunn. "I was so disappointed about not being able to go home that I had decided to stay in my room and cry all day."

"You can count on me," said Mr. Willis. He worked on the *Tribune* and had planned to hurry away after dinner and attend the football game with two or three other young newspapermen. But for the last month or so it had been growing upon Mr. Willis just how pretty and sweet little Miss Dunn was, and this seemed a splendid chance to get better acquainted with her.

"Well, I haven't anywhere else to go, so I guess *I'll* be here all right," said Miss Dempsey. Plain, blunt, middle-aged Miss Dempsey was a secretary in one of the flour mills.

"It's most kind of you to ask me," said the fourth boarder with the slow, gentle courtesy that fitted so well with his white hair and frock coat, "but I am afraid that unless…" He hesitated. "My nephew is to be in town for Thanksgiving Day. I just received word this morning, and I wondered if it would be a great imposition—"

"We'd be glad to have him come, too," Mrs. Martin said cordially.

Mr. Thompson beamed.

"We will be happy to come," he said.

"Kathleen," her mother protested when the three Martins were in the kitchen, washing the dinner dishes, "I wish you had let me see those invitations first. What on earth did you ask them all to spend the afternoon for? It was all right to make the dinner a party, but an ill-assorted group like that will be as restless as witches before the day is over."

"Why, Mother!" Kathleen's dish towel paused reproachfully in mid-air. "Who ever heard of people's leaving a party the minute dinner is over! They're not a bit more ill-assorted than most of our family parties."

"Besides," said Lois, coming to her sister's support, "we said, 'if there is nothing else that you want to do.' If they think they're going to be bored they needn't stay."

"Well, there's no helping it now, anyway," said Mrs. Martin philosophically. She paused a moment, "I wonder what Mr. Thompson's nephew is like?"

"I'll bet he's a fashionable young bachelor," said Lois. "Mr. Thompson has quite a lot of money and—"

"I'll bet he wears spats," was Kathleen's contribution. "I'm glad we thought of having coffee in front of the fire. He'll see that we're not so slow ourselves."

47

Thanksgiving breakfast was a light, hasty meal.

"We wouldn't eat anything, anyhow," said Mr. Willis. "We don't want to cramp our style for dinner."

The party was bringing an element of personality into the pleasant formality that had been the atmosphere of the house.

"Oh, I *hope* it will snow!" said Kathleen, scanning the cloudy sky. "It would seem so much more Thanksgiving-y."

"We nearly always had sleighing for Thanksgiving at home in New Hampshire," said Miss Dempsey.

After breakfast Mr. Willis departed for the office. Mr. Thompson left for the station to meet his nephew, and the two women went upstairs to their rooms. Then the folding doors between the dining room and the living room were closed, and from that time on in the back part of the house preparation ruled supreme.

Mrs. Martin moved briskly from table to refrigerator, from sink to stove. At 10:00 she put the turkey into the oven. Lois deftly made butter balls, washed lettuce, and chopped nuts. But it was Kathleen who kept up the spirit of the party.

"Oh, girls! Look!" she called, watching with rapt eyes the few feathery flakes that were sifting down upon the hard brown ground. "There!" she said. "Now just come and see if this table doesn't look lovely."

At either end, hollowed pumpkins were filled with shining apples and oranges, grapes, and bananas. The place cards, yellow chrysanthemums painted by Lois, waved from the tops of the tall slender glasses. And scattered about the table in holders of cardboard and gilded walnut shells were dozens of little candles waiting to be lighted.

"Why, Kathie, it's lovely!"

"And cheap!" Kathleen said eagerly. "It didn't cost a penny except for the candles. The walnut shells came from the nuts in the mincemeat; the pumpkins the boarders will eat later in pies that Mother will make of them."

Just at noon the doorbell rang, causing great excitement. It proved to be a box of flowers from one of Miss Dunn's admirers.

"Girls, look at these!" said Kathleen, coming back to the kitchen with her arms full of American Beauties. "Miss Dunn says we can have them for the dining room." She placed the two tall vases on the buffet. "There! That gives the whole thing tone. The nephew with the spats will give one glance at those, and he'll know this is no husking bee."

A little before 2:00, the nephew arrived. Lois was the first to see him. She clutched Kathleen, and the two peered through the crack in the double door. He was a tall, awkward, freckle-faced boy of 16 or so. The girls stared for a moment, then retreated to the kitchen for a hysterical outburst.

"A fashionable bachelor!" gasped Lois.

"Did you notice any sp-spats?" said Kathleen.

At quarter past two the dining-room curtains were drawn, the three dozen little yellow candles lighted, and the doors flung open. There was a delighted gasp from the five guests.

It was a most successful party. The boarders had put on their holiday moods with their holiday clothes. In a soft blue silk dress, Miss Dempsey did not seem half so much the brusque, reserved business woman. And little Miss Dunn, in her straight black velvet dress with its lace collar, with her wide blue eyes and her yellow hair, curling softly against her creamy neck, made a picture from which Mr. Willis could hardly take his eyes. He told funny stories of newspaper life and bandied jokes with Mr. Thompson with a geniality that would have made any party "go." Mr. Thompson watched Bobby Smith at first, eager for his sister's boy to have a good time and appear to advantage. He soon dropped all responsibility there, however, when he found him stealing almonds from Kathleen's cup and telling Lois about a football game.

With one exception, they were the same people who gathered at the same table twice a day. Now instead of a businesslike boardinghouse dinner prepared for pay was the gracious atmosphere of a feast prepared for love. It showed in Mrs. Martin's "best" dress, that gracious spirit, in the alligator-pear salad and in the candied orange peel; it twinkled in the tiny yellow candles and chuckled in the silly little conundrums written on the backs of the place cards. It was the spirit of hospitality that brings forth its best for guests.

When they had eaten the last bit of mince pie and the last little candle had flickered out, it was after 4:00. According to plan, they all went into the living room to drink their coffee 'round the snapping wood fire.

"I'm glad we saved all these berry boxes from canning time," said Kathleen, putting on another armful. "They burn up in a minute, but don't they make the most thrilling fire!"

The feathery snowflakes had changed to a cold autumn rain that blew against the windows. Twilight fell early; the firelight flickered, leaving shadowy corners in the living room. After a bit, words came fitfully; there were little periods of silence.

Kathleen, in her place on the floor beside the fire, ceased poking idly at the wood. Sensitive, responsive, she had caught the strange, wistful solemnity that so often steals down on holiday evenings. She leaned back against her mother's knee.

"It seems sort of—sort of ghostly, doesn't it?" she said in a hushed tone.

Then the ghosts stole in, the ghosts of other and different Thanksgivings.

"How well I remember the first Thanksgiving after we came west," said Mr. Thompson. "It was the year after the Indian trouble. Minneapolis was St. Anthony Falls then."

It was a story of pioneer days that he told, of raw country, of hardships and successes. Then Miss Dunn told of the first year that she had taught school in the New Hampshire hills and of their having been snowed in the day before Thanksgiving and having to stay until Friday morning with nothing to eat but what was left in the children's luncheon baskets. Mrs. Martin told of a Thanksgiving when, as a bride and fledgling housekeeper, she had had to entertain wealthy friends of her husband's.

When the clock struck eight, it was like a signal summoning them from the past. Miss Dunn straightened up suddenly.

"Please, Mrs. Martin," she said, "we've recovered from our feasting. Please let us all help do the dishes."

"Oh, no, we'll do them after—" Mrs. Martin began.

"After we've gone home, you were going to say," Miss Dunn accused her. "But we're already at home, you see; so there's no chance of our going. Please!"

Mr. Willis was already on his way to the dining room.

"This is a heaven-sent opportunity," he said. "I've always wondered whether all this newfangled domestic science amounted to anything. We have a domestic science teacher at our mercy, and we'll see if she really knows how to wash dishes."

The Martin kitchen that night was a hilarious place. At the sink, Mr. Willis, with a gingham apron tied about his neck, washed dishes. Kathleen presided over another pan on the table; Lois and Bobby Smith raced to see who should wipe each plate and cup as it came from the hot rinsing water. Miss Dunn wiped the dishes that Mr. Willis washed, and, judging from her occasional laughter and blushes, acquaintance was progressing quite as fast as well. There was much rivalry between the two teams, much good-natured bandying back and forth that ended with Mr. Willis's seizing Lois and depositing her high and dry upon the top of the refrigerator, where he left her until he and Miss Dunn had caught up with the rival team.

At last they all went back to the living room for a little music. Miss Dunn played, and Lois and Kathleen went out to the cabinet in the hall in search of some old books of music. They stole a moment for congratulations. Kathleen seized her sister about the waist.

"Honestly, hasn't this been the nicest holiday party we've ever had!"

"Everybody has been so nice," said Lois. "Wasn't it dandy of Mr. Thompson to invite us all to the theater tomorrow night in honor of his nephew? I haven't been to the theater in a decent seat since the Consolidated failed."

"They were all so nice," said Kathleen. "The idea of Miss Dunn's saying she'd just love to help me make over my pink dress! I like even Miss Dempsey. Do you know," she went on eagerly, "I believe it was because we were pretending we really wanted them here that they seemed so nice. We didn't keep kind of—kind of resenting them all the time."

"But the funny part is," Lois admitted in a whisper, "it wasn't pretending at all after the first. Why, when we were all fooling in the kitchen, I suddenly thought how glad I was that it wasn't going to end like most parties—everybody go home, and it's over with a bang—that they'd all be here for breakfast in the morning and for dinner tomorrow night and right on."

"I know it," said Kathleen eagerly. "Of course, it's a lot more work, and home isn't the same, but I think it's going to be real fun having them here."

"They probably won't always seem quite so nice as they do tonight," said Lois sagely. "They're at their best today. But then—"

There was a little pause in the music; then from the living room came soft, familiar notes:

Mid pleasures and palaces though we may roam,

Be it ever so humble, there's no place like home.

One voice after another took up the old tune, Mr. Thompson's a bit quavery, Miss Dempsey's a bit off key.

In the shadowy hall Kathleen's arm tightened 'round her sister. Where the light from the living room fell, she could see the rug over which they had all walked so many happy days, the corner of the case where their favorite books were kept; she knew what was in the shadowy corner—the hat rack with their mother's coat and umbrella, the clock that had ticked so loud in the stillness the night their father died, the window seat where their mother stopped to wave good-bye to them when they started off for school. It all seemed suddenly, poignantly sweet. Perhaps some Thanksgiving—

The plaintive melody went on. Kathleen's eyes suddenly filled with impulsive tears.

"Think of their singing that anywhere but home!" she said, with her voice choking a little.

"I know it," said Lois. "I was just thinking that, too. I'm—oh, I don't care if the Consolidated did fail—I'm so glad we've got the house and each other!"

"And honestly," said Kathleen, laughing shakily, "I'm thankful that we've got the boarders. If we can somehow manage to make it seem like home to them, too—"

The last flicker had died out in the fireplace; the little, old-fashioned grate with its narrow hearthstone was black and dead. But the spirit that kindles all home fires was burning bright. And in the magic of that Thanksgiving night, the hearth where only three had gathered had suddenly grown wide.

A kind man benefits himself...

PROVERBS 11:17

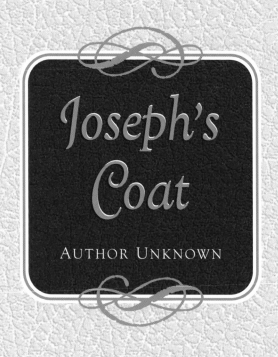

Joseph's Coat

AUTHOR UNKNOWN

Aunt Caroline sent
Joseph a coat — a warm coat.
But it had a flaw, and
the minister's son found it.

It was nipping cold for November. Winter had arrived before schedule.

"My, this coat feels good!" Joseph gave a little flying leap to express how good it felt. His thin legs seemed to lose themselves upward, his happy face, mounted on a thin little neck, to lose itself downward in the huge new coat.

Mother was happy today, too, as she watched him down the road. *Nobody will look at his back,* she thought. *They'll just look at his face, and say, "My, that boy's warm, I know!"*

But somebody looked at his back. At the junction of the roads, a little way on, the minister's boy and his particular friends swung in behind Joseph. They were all warm, too. The minister's boy's coat was new, too, but a different "new" from Joseph's. It had a fur collar that turned up—up—about his ears, and it was exactly broad enough and long enough.

All at once somebody shouted. It was the minister's boy.

"Oh, look! Joseph's coat—Joseph's coat of many colors!" Then the others took it up. "Joseph's coat of many colors! Looker there! Looker there!"

Suddenly Joseph was no longer warm; a nipping cold struck through to his small vitals.

"Joseph's coat! Joseph's coat!"

He knew there was something the matter with it, and it must be with the—the behind of it, for that was all those boys could see. All the leap had come out of Joseph's thin little legs, all the joy out of his heart. He went on because you couldn't get to school without going on. But that was all—just went on.

At the schoolhouse he waited around, instinctively facing front to folks, until they had all gone in. Then he took off his "new" coat, and looked at the behind. Then he knew.

There was a long straight seam in the middle, and on each side of it the thick cloth had faded to a different shade, a distinctly different shade. Two colors really, one on each side of that long straight seam—a cruel little trick of the sun. Joseph was only eight, but he saw at once why they had called it Joseph's coat of many colors. It *was* Joseph's coat of many colors.

The next day Joseph waited behind a wall at the junction of roads until the minister's boy and his particular friends had come and gone. Then he slipped out and followed them. That helped a little—he tried to think it helped a little. But there were recesses and noonings—of course he might stay in recesses and noonings; you don't have to wear an over-coat when you stay in.

Joseph stayed in. Through the window he could see the minister's boy's new coat having a splendid time. The third day he saw something else. He saw the minister's boy in *his* coat—the one Aunt Caroline sent— strutting about the yard amid the other's shouts of delight. Some of the others tried it on and strutted. Joseph just sat in his seat and looked at them.

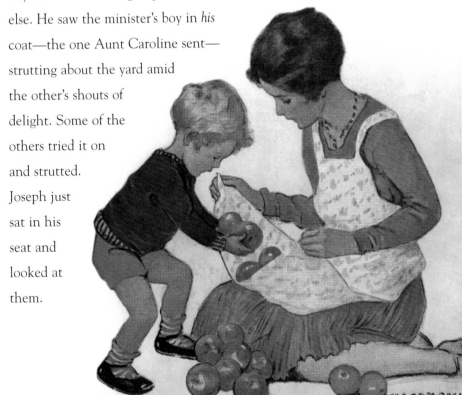

The next day he turned Aunt Caroline's coat inside out, and wore it so. He waited till he got nearly to the fork in the road, and then turned it; he wasn't going to make Mother feel bad too. She had lined the coat anew with shiny black cotton stuff all of one color. Joseph felt a little better; this would help.

But it only made things worse. The minister's boy and his particular friends instantly saw the ridiculousness of that inside-out little coat. "Look at it! Look at it—inside out! Wearin' it inside out!" The joke was just too good!

There was just one other thing to do, and Joseph did it the next day. The place where the roads forked was about halfway from Joseph's home to the schoolhouse; so he went warm halfway the next day. The other half he shivered along, very small indeed, and very cold indeed, outside of the Aunt Caroline coat. For he had left Aunt Caroline's coat folded up behind a stone wall. Going home that afternoon, he was warm the last half of his way, anyway. It helped to be half warm.

For a day or two the sun and the wind conspired together to befriend little Joseph. But the fourth day the wind blew and the sun rested. There was snow, too, in fine steely flakes, and Joseph's teeth chattered, and he ran on stiff little legs, and blew on stiff little fingers. He kept looking ahead to the last half of going home. He wished he had pushed the Aunt Caroline coat farther in under the stones out of the way of the snow.

"Joseph Merriam," called the teacher on the day after the snowstorm. She had her roll book and pencil waiting, but she got no answer. It was strange for Joseph Merriam not to answer the roll call; he was one of her little steadies.

"Joseph is not here, I see; can anyone tell me if he is sick? He must be sick."

"Yes'm, he is. He's got the pneumonia dreadfully," someone answered. "There were lights in his house all night, my father said."

For many nights there were lights, and for many mornings the doctor's sleigh. Joseph lay in his bed, saying wild, mixed-up words in a weak little voice.

"I'm most to the stone wall; then I'll be warm!"

"Joseph's coat o' many colors—Joseph's coat o' many colors!"

"I don't want Mother to know they laughed; don't anybody tell Mother."

The minister's boy heard of those wild little words, and pieced them together into a story. He remembered who had cried, "Joseph's coat o' many colors!" tauntingly, cruelly. And now—oh, now he remembered that Joseph had not worn any overcoat at all those last days that he went to school! *No coat.* The heart of the minister's boy contracted with an awful fear. He took to haunting Joseph's home in all his free minutes—waiting at the gate for the doctor to come out, and shivering with something besides cold at his brief answers. The answers grew worse and worse....

Every night the minister's boy was glad to go to bed and try to forget. But going to bed was not going to sleep. One night he lay in his own bed, remembering that other little bed of Joseph's. When remembering was too great a torture, the minister's boy crept out of bed and dressed himself. Out into the clear, cold starlight, down the frozen road, he crept toward Joseph's lighted windows. He was not sensible of being cold anywhere but in his soul—he shivered there.

A long time he stood waiting for he knew not what. Then someone came out of the house. It was not the doctor; it was the minister. The boy could not see his face, but you don't have to see your own father's face. They went back down the dim night road together, and together into the minister's study.

"I've killed him," the boy said. "I've killed Joseph. I did it."

The minister's face was curiously lighted in spite of this awful confession of his son. The light persisted.

"Sit down, Philip," he said, for the boy was shaking like a leaf. "Now tell me."

All the story, piece by piece—the boy told it all.

"So it was I—I killed him. I—I didn't *expect* to—"

Silence for a little. Then:

"Did you think Joseph was dead, Philip? He came very close indeed to it; but the crisis is past, and he will get well. I waited to know."

"You mean—I—*haven't?*"

"I mean you haven't, thank God. Kneel down with me and thank Him." Father and son knelt together, their hearts overflowing with glad thanksgiving praises.

When, after a long while, the boy was slipping away, the minister called to him gently.

"Come back a moment, Philip."

"Yes, I'm back, Father. I know what you're thinking of. Father, may I—punish myself this time—for making fun of a boy—a *little* boy? It needs a good deal o' punishin', but I'll do it—please let me do it, Father! Please—please *try* me, anyway."

And because the minister was a wise minister, he nodded his head.

When little Joseph got well, he wore to school a beautiful warm coat with a soft furry collar that went up—up—around his ears. It was very thick and warm and handsome, and all of a color. Joseph wore it all the way.

The rest of the winter the minister's boy wore to school an Aunt Caroline coat of many colors.

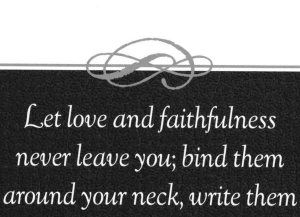

Let love and faithfulness
never leave you; bind them
around your neck, write them
on the tablet of your heart.

PROVERBS 3:3